P9-CCQ-914

Library of Congress Cataloging-in-Publication Data available.

ISBN 978-1-7972-1166-4

Manufactured in the United States of America.

Design by Indya McGuffin.
Art Direction by Amelia Mack.
Typeset in Mr Eaves.
The illustrations in this book were rendered in colored pencil.

10 9 8 7 6 5 4 3 2 1

Chronicle Books LLC
680 Second Street
San Francisco, California 94107

www.chroniclekids.com

For Charlie and August, of course, and
everyone who helped light the way

—TT

To Kayla, for everything

—GS

# There Is a Rainbow

Written by
Theresa Trinder

Pictures by
Grant Snider

chronicle books · san francisco

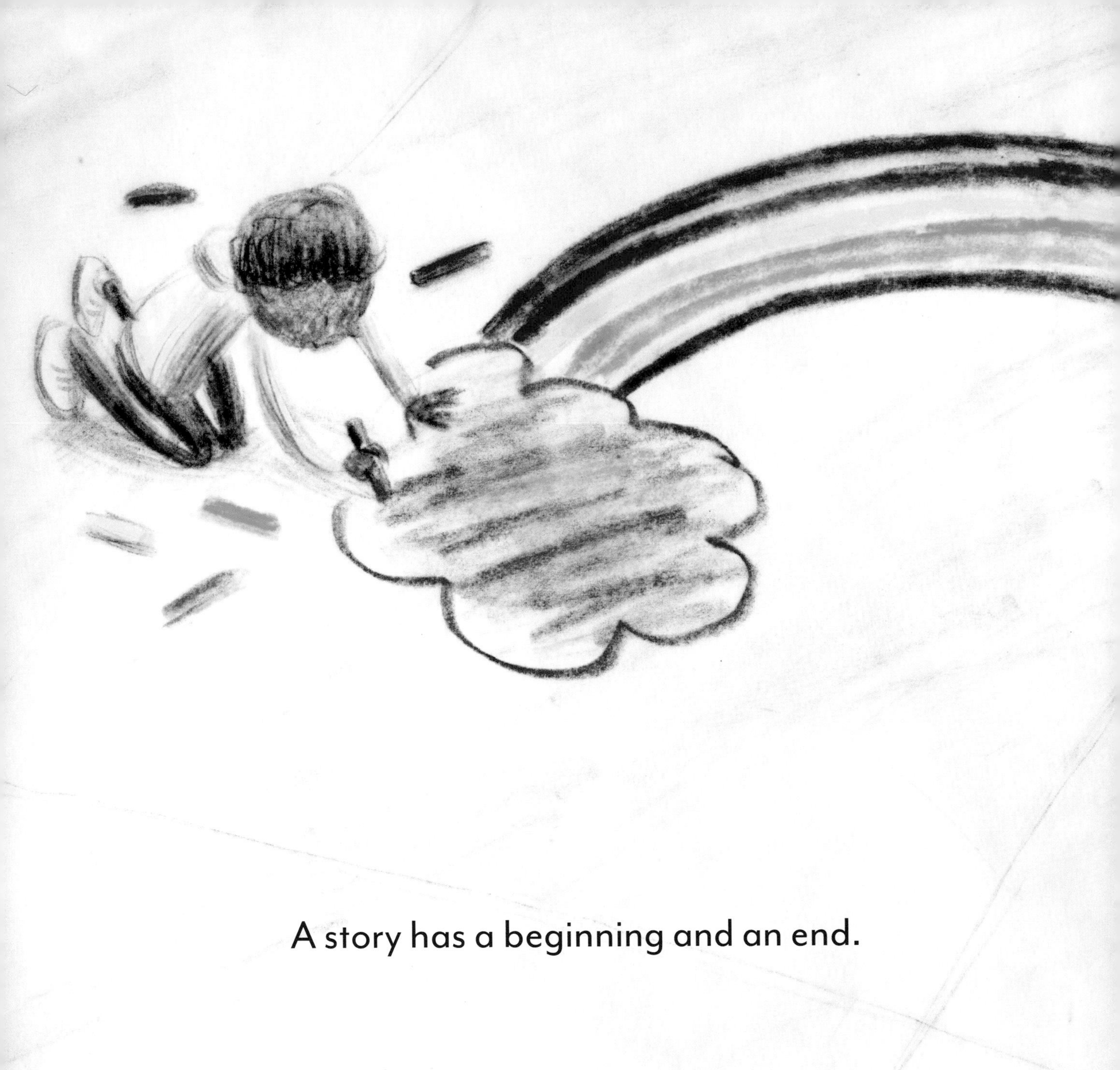

A story has a beginning and an end.

There is a here. There is a there.

And there is something in between.

On the other side of the screen

there is a school.

On the other side

of a window

BLACK LIVES MATTER
BLACK FUTURES MATTER
We got this!
STAY SAFE

there is a neighbor.

On the other side of the street

there is help.

BLACK
LIVES
MATTER

On the other side of town

there is a voice.

On the other side of a river

there is light.

On the other side of a mountain

there is a path.

On the other side of sadness

there are hugs.

On the other side

of a storm

there is a rainbow.

On the other side

of today

there is tomorrow.

WE MISSED
YOU

THANK YOU HEROES
STAY SAFE
HOPE
STAY STRONG

## Author's Note

In the spring of 2020, I wrote this book while staying home with my family to help stop the spread of COVID-19. There was loss. There was fear. But there were children. And all over the world, they painted rainbows in their windows and drew messages on the ground to remind the world that we are in this together.

My boys wanted to bring a rainbow to their grandmother, but they were struggling with social distancing. So I put on the mask and gloves and delivered their rainbow myself. I held my mom's hand a moment, then called from the car: "See you on the other side."

I thought: We *will* see each other on the other side. Yes, there are sad goodbyes. But there will be joyous reunions. And even though we can't reach out and touch one another right now, we can see one another—truly see one another—if we try.

It comforts me to think of families reading this book a year—or many years—from now and to hope they're looking back on this time from a place that is safer, happier, more generous, and more just.

I wonder if the rainbows will still hang in the windows.

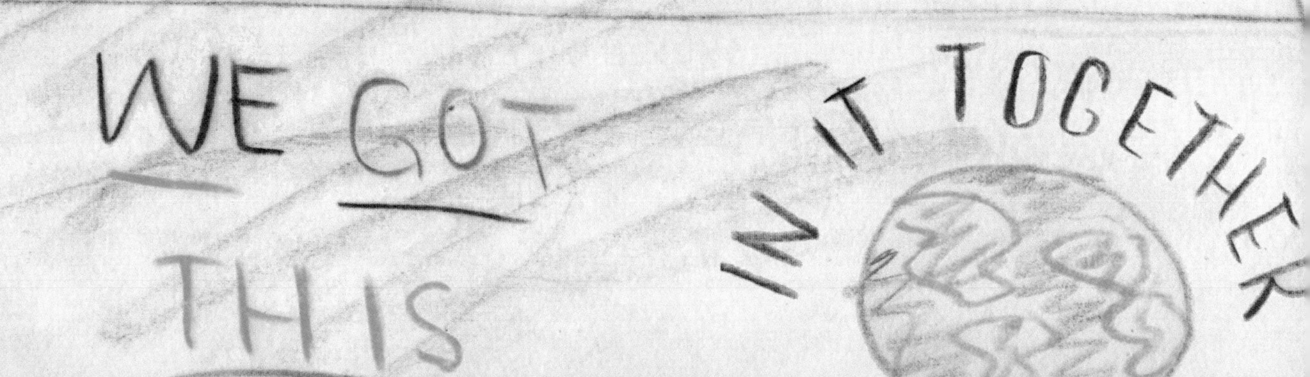